What people are saying . . . .

"In an era before most horseplayers bet with a computer or a smartphone, racetracks were among the most colorful places on earth, filled with wise guys and hustlers and an assortment of characters looking to make a fast buck. John Scheinman's *Bal Harbour Blues*, set in Miami in 1991, evokes these memorable days. John has a Runyonesque feel for the lingo of the racetrack, and an irrepressible affection for even the crooks and con men who populate it. I loved this story."

— Andrew Beyer, author of *Picking Winners*

"What do you do when you get an offer from Louie the Finger that you can't refuse? Unless you believe that a lead pipe against the side of your head is beneficial to your health and happiness, you take it. John Scheinman has crafted a novella as funny as it is literate."

— Jerry Izenberg, Hall of Fame sports columnist

"If you like plain-spoken, hard-boiled pulp fiction written by Mickey Spillane, Dashiell Hammett, and Raymond Chandler, you will love *Bal Harbour Blues*. In a spot-on noir voice, his story of scams, numbers and racing goes deep, as it's also about family, love, and trust, with a touch of humor in all the right places."

— Sass _____ of
_____ _ality

Bal Harbour Blues

by

John Scheinman

Lost Valley Press

Cover Photo: Andre Jenny / Alamy Stock Photo

ISBN: 978-1-935874-41-6 print
ISBN: 978-1-935874-42-3 eBook

Lost Valley Press
An Imprint of Satya House Publications
POB 122
Hardwick, MA 01037

Acknowledgements

Thanks to my sister Julie Murkette, the family book publisher and editor, who midwifed this novella; Eric Bottjer; Ryan Goldberg; Professor Joe Tinkelman; my brother Andrew; sister Nancy; and my late grandfather Tony, who said his friends were all in Sing Sing.

1

Bal Harbour, Florida, 1991 — Why did I agree to come back to Florida? I mean, I'm fifty-five not seventy-five, and it's not like I'm itching to spend the rest of my life doing battle with the claimers at Calder or die of a stroke watching Jai alai. They're putting me out to pasture here. Sixty-five grand a year and the condo are fine, I guess, but a man has got to live.

Louie the Finger calls me up at 3 o'clock in the morning . . . on a Sunday.

"Johnny, we're pulling you out."

"Louie," I say. "My numbers are running 20,000 strong a week. My clients have got more faith in me than the pope. And what are you calling at 3 o'clock for?"

"The rates are cheaper. And by the way, I can sign you up for MCI's Friends and Family program. It'll save me twenty dollars a month."

Can you believe this guy? Louie the Finger controls the whole fucking world, and, as if that's not enough, his fat Ethel Merman daughter owns the only deli in Queens selling Parma prosciutto for $12.99 a pound for which the whole neighborhood treats them like God and lines up around the block. I mean it's not like Louie needs a better phone plan.

When I hang up, my wife, Eleanor, rolls over in bed and asks me why they call him Louie the Finger. I've known this guy forty-five years and now she's asking this question? At 3 o'clock in the morning? On a Sunday? It's not like she's going to let me go back to sleep if I don't answer.

"It was like this, Eleanor," I say, propping myself up. "In 1950, Louie Fracarro is playing the horses at Hialeah and losing his shirt. Louie and Carla, the DeVitos, Big Al Raymond and his wife, my parents and I are all spending a month down there. I was in short pants, but I knew my way around the racetrack.

"So, one day Louie's deep in the Daily Racing Form, mapping out a double. It's getting close to post time, and he's frantic. Big Al's next to him, drunk off his ass, and he takes out a pastrami sandwich he's got in a brown bag, like a little kid's school lunch. He's cutting it in half with a Swiss Army Knife, when Louie suddenly jumps out of his chair screaming, 'I got it!'

"Big Al turns around with his pastrami sandwich and Swiss Army Knife and accidentally cuts off Louie's right index finger. How does a Swiss Army Knife get that fucking sharp, right?

"Anyway, the track announcer calls two minutes to post. Louie, blood gushing out of the finger hole, heads for the window. Then, out of nowhere, a flamingo swoops down, grabs the bloody digit off the bench, and flies away. Jimmy DeVito yells, 'Louie, the finger!' But it was too late. The flamingo flaps onto the infield lake, and from our seats we watch it stretch its neck and choke down the finger. And that's how he got the name Louie the Finger."

"You're joking."

"No, Eleanor. It's 3 o'clock in the morning. I'm not joking. And if you think that's unbelievable, we didn't even leave the track. After the first race, Louie goes to the first aid room there and comes back with a roll of gauze. In the second race, Louie watches his long shot win by seven while squeezing this bloody fucking gauze ball over his hand. The bet pays like $400 and Louie uses the money to buy himself a hard rubber fake finger to attach to his hand."

"You're serious."

"It looks real, you know? But I get the creeps even giving him a handshake. That rubber finger doesn't curl around your hand with the rest of the fingers."

"You're joking."

"I'm telling you, he's got a rubber finger."

"Go back to sleep, John."

Three weeks later, Eleanor and I are in Florida.

"Johnny, look at this place. It's beautiful."

Everywhere you look — marble. It's like the men's room at Caesar's.

"Eleanor, half these people are dead."

"You mean they're half dead."

"It's a fucking mausoleum."

"I think it's beautiful. They didn't have a place like this back on Atlantic Avenue. Do you have to be so negative all the time?"

2

Florida wasn't my idea. I'm having lunch with Eddie the Fixer at Bamonte's in Brooklyn, and we're demolishing clams casino.

"Feel free to explain, Eddie, how it's going to look for me, hanging around doing nothing?"

"Louie said the same thing."

"Why aren't I surprised?"

"Hey, it's not a negative. Facts aren't political. A condo on the beach in Florida is nice in the winter, John."

"Florida?"

"Why don't you ask Eleanor what she thinks?"

"Eddie, come on. What's that?"

"Just saying, John, and you get the pension."

The pasta comes out. Eddie and I, we've eaten here a thousand times, and it's always the same, and the place is ours. No riffraff.

"Could you go to Florida, Eddie?" I said, shoving a meatball in my mouth.

"When it's time, John, don't we all?"

When I get home, I tell Eleanor we're moving, and she jumps into my arms like we're crossing the threshold. I kind of want to do it when she's like this, but the meatballs are sitting in my chest, and I need to put her down.

Sixty-five grand a year. Not bad, I guess, for doing nothing, right? Plus, Grant's Tomb here. I also got a half-million in the bank, but I like working. I don't really want Louie's pension. We were doing fine the way things were in New York. But it's like friggin' Wall Street up there now. They're profit crazy.

You're making one million, they want two million. You make two million, they want four million. These people are never satisfied. Don't get me wrong, I believe in making money, but see how you feel when it's your job they got no use for anymore. We were doing fine with the numbers. Nobody complained. Now they're going to sell crack in there? I don't think so. My people don't smoke crack. They're hard-working people, family people. What the hell do they want to mess with that street scum for all of a sudden? Those drug people don't have any money. They're fucking crack addicts.

"Johnny. Don't look, but that woman just fell over on her walker."

"Jesus Christ, Eleanor."

"Do you think there's any people our age living here?"

"If we stay here long enough, there will be."

"Johnny, let's go up and break in the new bed. OK?"

Eleanor had brought the pillows and old blankets from Queens. I don't care what people tell you, not everything is supposed to change. You want to keep me happy? Don't change anything until I'm dead.

"Come here, big boy," Eleanor said with that mouth.

I still can't believe how I met her. We're having a big family dinner at my cousin Angela's in Flatbush. I'm just 19, you know? A backwards kid. I had a few girls in the car after school when we couldn't control ourselves, but that was it. They send me out to pick up the meat for dinner. I walk down to Martinelli's butcher shop on 49th and there she is behind the counter.

I'd never seen anything like Eleanor. Three years older than me, sweat pouring off her brow, shirt wet, top buttons open, hands covered in blood. She looked like the Angel of Death after just finishing off the first-born Jews. Big head of black hair pinned up. Big chest. Big, beautiful eyebrows. Big, red mouth.

Jesus Christ, I got a hard-on just looking at her. She had this crazy look when she was in the shop. Like she'd reached the point where she could hack up anything, anybody, at any moment. Just put your hand on the wood block and she'll chop it right off for you. Like she could cut a hunk out of your head, weigh it, and wrap it right up.

'Here's your head, Mrs. Faiella, half-price today. $7.99 a pound.'

So, she's squeezing this long, sharp knife in those slick bloody hands, looks me over and says in the sweetest, toughest voice you ever heard, "What can I do for you?"

I ordered fourteen veal chops, just staring.

"You like watchin' me chop up the meat?"

"Sure. Sure," I said like an idiot. "You look great doing it. I mean, you look like an expert chopping up meat."

"You wanna try?"

"You wanna go out with me?"

"I thought you were here for veal."

Eleanor was like a bottomless well of fire. She was insatiable. The back seat. The front seat. The kitchen counter. The kitchen floor. On the bed. Under the bed. The closet. The staircase. The ironing board. The butcher shop. One night she wanted to try it standing on our heads. So, she took off her clothes and put her head down on the floor and flipped herself up with her back facing the wall and said, "Fuck me."

I disappointed her, you know? Not everything turns me on, I'm sorry to say, and I didn't want to fuck Eleanor upside down. But that was the nice thing about her. She didn't drag anything out. If things weren't going the way she wanted, she'd shift directions and be on to something else. I liked that. She never wanted to fight, and neither did I.

"Johnny," she said one night. "Don't you think all the people getting divorced in the world could try having a little more fun with each other? Don't you think that's the problem? Nobody's having enough fun."

"You're not exactly a barrel of laughs either, you know, Eleanor."

And she punched me in the stomach with a straight left and then jumped on me and started tickling.

"I'll show you who's not fun, you bastard."

"Uncle, Eleanor! Uncle!"

After a while, I didn't want Eleanor in the store anymore. Men leering at her while she chops up the meat. It's disgusting. My wife should be at home. I called Charlie Martinelli one day. I says, "Charlie, Eleanor's through."

He says, "What do you mean, through? Eleanor is the butcher shop."

Eleanor didn't like me getting jealous. She thought we needed the money and she liked to work. She's yelling and screaming at me that night. I went out. Slammed the door and went downtown. I hit some fucking guy coming out of the subway. Punched him right in the mouth and felt his teeth fold in. He cracked his head on the steps there. I never hit a guy with so much money before. It was like punching a slot machine. He must have had two thousand dollars. His ring slid off like he had a girl's hand. I brought it home to Eleanor as a gift. She lit up like a Christmas tree. "Oh, Johnny, you shouldn't have."

"Put your coat on, baby," I said. "We're going out."

3

I was pulling forty grand a week when the state lottery suddenly starts offering every game you can think of except three-card Monty. They even made a game called Numbers. That's what we call it! Why not just hire us to run the fucking business, right? Screw New York. People like our numbers better, anyway. We actually pay out more, you can bet on credit and by phone. We even let kids play.

Numbers — our numbers — are adjunct business at this point. Supplemental. We've been diversified for a long time. Rental property. Construction. Jersey Shore board-walks. Trucks. Taxis. Lots of service economy rackets, but no drugs and no prostitutes, at least not until now. Numbers? We didn't steal that from somebody else. That's an Italian game.

I'm strictly a numbers guy, and I ran all of Staten Island and parts of Brooklyn. I had about twenty-five little strong-arm hoodlums running around for me collecting money and numbers. High school kids. Girls even, snapping bubblegum when they showed up with their bags of money. I'd say, "Girls, please. This is a professional operation. Lose the gum."

One time a girl looks at me when I say this and blows a bubble so large it blocks out her entire face. She takes it out of her mouth, hands it to me and walks away laughing. But that's moxie, right? That was about as far as disrespect went. I preferred working with kids. They appreciated the opportunity.

Nobody else their age is making that kind of money.

Adults get lost, cutting side deals, looking to undermine your authority, backtalking, getting lazy, maybe trying to take over or even kill you. Kids never get tired, love to play tough guy, and will do anything if you give them a hundred bucks. I just tell them, "Keep your mouth shut."

Then, for emphasis, I tell them this story I made up about a guy I had to kill because he was talking about business.

"You ever heard of Frank Anderson?" I asked when I thought a kid was losing track of responsibilities. "He was the best runner I ever had. Pulled in more money than all you kids put together. You know what a Rolls Royce is? You know what an Eldorado is? He drove those cars and ate lobster and steak every night and was married to a girl who once starred in a porno movie. But you know what happened to Frank? Frank had his fingernails pulled out by two tiny Asian ladies in a nail spa I own. Then you know what happened to Frank? Frank had his bleeding fingers dipped in a bowl of spicy hot Chinese mustard. Then you know what happened to Frank? Frank drank two gallons of water but never took a piss. And do you know why Frank never took a piss? Because after he drank all that water, Frank had his mouth stuffed with live eels and his head blown off his neck by the biggest fucking gun you ever saw in your life. Would you like to make me unhappy? Because I like to indulge that side of my creativity, and I'm sure I can think of plenty wonderful things to do to you, too."

Sometimes I would drive a kid out to Calvary Cemetery. That's a spooky place with maybe three million people buried in it. Crazy old gothic headstones and cracked statues of angels and crumbling mausoleums packed in like a graveyard city that stretches all the way to the Empire State Building, which rises up in the distance like the biggest tombstone of all. There must be a hundred Frank Andersons in Calvary.

So they know I'm not kidding, I take some nervous squirt out there around 7 o'clock, a scary time in a cemetery with night coming, to show them where he is buried. To tell the truth, I don't even like walking through there myself at that hour. You start picturing your own coffin, or your parents and grandparents suffocating underground in a box, just skeletons. You feel like some dead Irishman from the 1800s is going to come jumping out from behind a stone. I'm getting chills, so I know the kid wants to go home.

One time I took this punk into Calvary to put the fear in him, and we walked to the center of the cemetery and up to a Frank Anderson headstone, and I said, "There's where he's buried without his head," and the kid turns to me and says, "That thing says he died in 1914. You're a liar."

"Smart kid," I said, like an idiot. "Let's get out of here. You passed the test."

My father was a guy everybody called Uncle Al and it seemed like he never worked a day in his life. When I was a kid, it was confusing for me to have everyone calling my father "Uncle." I'll never forget my Uncle Mike coming up to me one night at a backyard cookout and saying, "Where's your Uncle Al?"

We lived in Rosedale, in Queens, near Kennedy Airport. My father took me to the airport one day and said, "You see this? This used to be called Idlewild Point. We used to play out here when we were your age; your grandfather used to go fishing here when he was a kid. People used to go on vacation here." A big jet took off and I couldn't hear anything else he said.

Our house was two miles from Jamaica Race Course, which they tore down in 1960, and my father went to the track every morning when it was open in April and then in October. To me and my mother it was the most natural thing in the world. I thought it was his job and definitely where the money came from because it seemed like my mother never worked a day in her life either. She'd get me up and off to school in the morning, clean the house for a half-hour, then drive with her friends into New York to shop at Bonwit Teller. When she heard Donald Trump had knocked down Bonwit Teller to build one of his towers, she cried like she had lost a relative.

Big Al Raymond would come by our house around 7 o'clock in the morning wearing sweatpants and sneakers, with a racing form under one arm and a duffel bag under the other. My father would come downstairs looking just the same, and they'd head down the street, beating the jogging craze by about fifteen years. When they got to the track, they'd go behind a barn, change into nice suits, and make the rounds.

Big Al Raymond was the biggest guy I knew, probably 6-foot-5, 240 pounds. About the only time I heard him talk was inside the house. Outside, he was a silent Indian. He wanted to intimidate people, and talking, for a big man, is like tipping your hand at cards. He had perfected an air of quiet menace. When he wore a suit, he pulled down the brim of his fedora so you could hardly see his eyes. My father was almost fifteen years older than Big Al, but they did everything together. They were the two Al's, Uncle Al and Big Al.

Big Al would go a few days without shaving to look a little older, a little tougher. Unlike my father, who dropped out of high school, Big Al went to Queens College, and he could tell you everything about New York — Jacob Riis, the Vanderbilts — the whole history of the city.

One Sunday, our families are driving through Long Island City and Big Al starts telling us how the place used to be called Steinway Village and then went off on a jag about pianos. I liked it better when he talked about guns and even more when he showed them to me. Big Al owned one of the very first .44 magnums, and the first time he showed it to me, taking it out of the duffel bag, I felt like I was looking at the world's greatest magic trick.

"You know what, Johnny?" Big Al said to me when I was fourteen. "Whoever I point this at does whatever I tell them." Then he slowly turned the barrel in my direction. "Now go help your mother in the kitchen."

That year, I was out at the track with the two Al's every Saturday, but not in the morning, when they made their rounds. Only for the races.

Unlike most of the men I saw at the track, the two Al's hardly bet. They would eat hot dogs, clam chowder, drink beer, talk to people I didn't know, show me off, look at the horses in the paddock and then suddenly, at some point during the day, turn very serious.

"You sit here with your Uncle Al," my father would say, and go off to the betting window. I sat there with my brain twisting up, thinking about how my father, who everybody called Uncle Al, was calling Big Al my Uncle Al even though he wasn't even my uncle.

"No cheering," my father always said when he came back to our seats, and the two Al's both watched the race in silence through their binoculars. Even when the horses crossed the finish line, I had no idea what was happening, if they had lost or won. My father would stand up and say, "We're leaving when I come back," and he would walk quickly back to the window. A few times, I remember him saying after a race, "Tell your mother I'm going to be late," and Big Al would take me home.

By the time I was sixteen, I knew how the whole thing worked, the morning rounds, all of it.

One day, my father let me stick around after one of the losses. Big Al stayed, too. My father looked like he was having trouble holding in a lot of anger. Next to Big Al, he didn't look like much — curly black hair losing out to a bald spot, bird beak nose, and a wiry body with arm muscles that made me wish he looked stronger. But he packed a punch like a steel-tip shoe. My father knew how to beat the shit out of people.

We had a neighbor who had a party one night, and the cars from the guests filled up the block. One of them parked in front of our driveway, blocking my father's car. He didn't have plans to go anywhere that night, but it was the principle of the thing. We're sitting around watching TV, and he's getting up and down, up and down, off the couch to look out the window to see if the car was still there. Finally, my mother asked him to quit it and my father went outside and slammed the front door. Now, I was getting up and down going to the window. At about 11:30 a guy walked up in front of our house.

"Is this your car?" my father asked him.

"Yeah," the man said, and my father said, "Take off your shoes and give them to me."

The man was smart enough to recognize trouble. He took off his shoes and handed them over.

"Now get in your car and move it because you're blocking my driveway."

The man did as he was told, parked, and came back for his shoes. My father dropped him with one right hand, put the shoes down next to his bloody nose and walked back into the house.

"Why didn't we get invited to that party?"

So, after the race, my father says, "Al, we've got to go pay a visit. Johnny, you can come, too."

Now I knew something important was happening that had to do with growing up. I felt nervous, but Big Al Raymond made you feel like you had an edge no matter what you were getting into.

We walked through the grandstand, out of the clubhouse, and made our way around the perimeter of the track to the barns on the back side. We went to barn No. 22, and my father asked a Black kid giving a colt a sponge bath if Charlie Utz was around.

"Boss is cooling out Mayhem right now," the kid said.

Just then, Charlie Utz comes around the corner of the shed row leading the horse that had won the last race. As soon as he sees my father, he stops and stands still. Then he looks at Big Al Raymond.

"Just like the old Mayhem, huh Charlie?" my father says.

"I had no idea he was so sharp," Charlie Utz says. "The kid said he couldn't hold him."

Charlie Utz walked Mayhem into his stall, looked over at us, and pinned up a hay ball for the horse. Then he got an old pail, filled it with water from a hose and slid it under the door. Mayhem dropped his head and started drinking.

"Looks like it took a lot out of him," my father said.

"No, I think he came out of it fine," Charlie Utz said.

"No, I think it took a lot out of him. I think he needs a little something to get over the race. We got anything that maybe can help this horse?"

Big Al Raymond opened his duffel bag and pulled out a black leather case, like an overnight travel kit. He unzipped it and took out a vial and a syringe.

"Oh, he don't need none of that," Charlie Utz said, but didn't move to stop it. Big Al Raymond walked to the stall, opened the door and went inside with Mayhem. The horse kept its face in the water pail. Big Al pushed the needle into its neck, and Mayhem went down like a frozen stone. Charlie Utz gasped, but he couldn't even push a word out.

"I told you I thought the race took a lot out of him," my father said. "Next time, tell the kid to save a little something."

4

We're not in Florida three weeks and Eleanor is dressing like she was crowned Little Miss Sunshine 1968. All of a sudden, she's exploding like fireworks. Aqua. Fuchsia. Mauve. Jesus Christ, whatever happened to red and blue? She starts wearing her hair up in these flimsy scarves and dark sunglasses that get pointy at the corners. I said, "Eleanor, I wanna give you a kiss but I might poke my eye out."

She starts bringing home shirts for me to wear, crazy Hawaiian shirts, and sandals. And Cuban cigars. "These are illegal, Eleanor,"

I tell her, running a cigar under my nose. I got to admit they smelled pretty good.

"Since when did you start caring about legal?" she says, and I forget to ask her where she got them. I'm still agitated, but the sun and the heat and the whole Florida thing start working on me. It's been a long time since I was down here as a kid. Eleanor takes me out for stone crabs. I'm drinking cold beer out of a frosted mug. There's a pelican on the dock outside. I love pelicans, the way they fly maybe an inch off the water, gliding along like they're about to drop a bomb on the Japs. I start thinking about the flamingos at Hialeah.

The next day we go to the track, Gulfstream Park. I start to understand Eleanor's colors. Everybody looks like they're wearing pajamas. The track's great, but I slip back into a bad mood. There's nothing for me to do here but drink and gamble. I miss the action.

That night we're standing out on our balcony looking at the ocean, and the sun is disappearing behind us and the whole sky is lit up orange like heaven's on fire. Eleanor's drinking a Fresca and she gives me a fizzy kiss. We both laugh after taking a deep breath at the same time. She looks down. "You're wearing the sandals, Johnny."

"Yeah, Eleanor, I'm wearing the sandals."

She wraps her arms around my right arm and holds me. I love the way she smells. I love the way she talks to me about myself, even when I don't believe her. The last thing I want to do in my life is let Eleanor down. It's nice and simple, having a woman who thinks you're the greatest. If you fight anyway, it probably means you don't like yourself.

The sun finishes up and I feel sleepy. It's only 8 o'clock.

"You wanna watch TV, Johnny?"

"No, let's just go to bed."

Inside, it feels good. When we got down here, we bought this bed that cost $4,000;

firm, like I like it. Eleanor reaches up and turns out the light and then pushes back into me.

"That feels good, Johnny," she says, but I'm already just about out.

———————

Whatever it is tramples my dream like a rampaging elephant knocking down a circus tent. Maybe ten seconds pass, ten seconds to slide back into a dream of me and the other kids playing Spin the Bottle out in the shed before the next explosion hits. I'm sitting bolt upright in bed, and I don't even remember grabbing the gun under the pillow, but it's in my hand and I'm ready to kill someone.

Eleanor waltzes into the room with a tray of food like she's nursing an invalid.

"It's 12 o'clock, Johnny. You can't sleep your life away." Christ, I slept for fourteen hours. Another explosion, and Eleanor starts laughing.

"What the fuck?" I yell. She pulls back the curtain and the blinding sun comes in and a wrecking ball slowly swings back away from the building next door toward our window. There's a gaping hole in the wall facing us, and the ball is about to take out another chunk. My mind starts working. If they're taking down this building and making all this noise today, they're going to put up another building in its place and make a whole lot more noise for at least another two years. The ball swings and I watch it crash and destroy and feel my head explode.

Eleanor is laughing harder, opening the window so it gets even louder. Dust is blowing into the bedroom.

"Eat your baloney sandwich, John, and drink your juice."

Baloney for breakfast. What am I doing here? I miss New York badly at this moment. The ball hits and it's so loud I know I'm not going to be staying home today. Then the crane starts emitting that beeping back-up alarm noise. It's winding up another bomb. I'm looking at the crater in the wall and all I feel is angry.

I hear Eleanor singing, "*Just call me angel of the morning, baby/Just touch my cheeks before you leave.*" The giant ball moves in slow-motion and I'm having an out-of-body experience, that same feeling I get right before I hurt someone very badly.

"Fuck you!" I'm screaming and I get out of bed and throw the baloney sandwich out the window. The bread flies off like the used-up stage of a rocket, and the baloney lands on the side of the wrecking ball right before it smashes into the building. When the ball swings back, the baloney is gone.

"Eleanor, bring me my binoculars."

In New York, I had a place, and I had a purpose. I understood who I was, what my life was about, what my day was going to look like, and how much money I could make if

I did what I do the right way. I didn't care that we didn't have any kids because when I wasn't working, I didn't want to be with anybody but my wife. I liked the guys, sure, but I'm a homebody.

Florida was supposed to be easy living, but at this moment I feel like I'm coming apart. I feel like a boat with a hole going down. I don't know what the fuck I'm supposed to do when I get up or who the fuck I am. I can feel Eleanor's hand massaging my neck. I don't want anyone else touching me, ever. She's saying stuff in my left ear, all that stuff that calms me down, but in my right ear it's the ball and the beeping and the grinding metal and the jackhammers.

"I can't do this, Eleanor."

"No, Johnny, we're gonna make it work."

I get the binoculars in focus and there in the room with the hole in the wall is the baloney on the floor. That's a pretty good shot. "Look at this," I say, passing Eleanor the binoculars and pointing to where she should aim.

"These are good binoculars, John," she says, looking at the baloney. "Who did you steal them from?"

———•———

A week later we're living in the Sea Breeze, an Art Deco dump on Collins Avenue. I feel like we're sliding through the cracks on our way to becoming deranged, badly sunburned street people. Eddie asks why we moved out of the condo, and I tell him to just send us a check for the difference.

It's hot as hell in the Sea Breeze, with a beat-up air-conditioner in the window that hasn't cooled down anyone since 1965. The buzzing rotating fan on the night table makes me want to check into a mental institution. I start drinking a lot of beer and staring at the lamp. If there's a bug, I stare at that.

I barely notice Eleanor's trips out during the day getting longer and longer. I drift off after a few beers, feet up, stunned by the heat and the next thing I know she's dancing in the door and it's four, five hours later. She seems like the same Eleanor to me, nothing to get suspicious about.

She sits on my lap, straddling my legs, then leans in and gives me a big, wet kiss saying, "Hello, big boy," like she's Mae West. She's not criticizing that I'm plopped there like cat shit in a litter box, but I know I'm not looking too good.

"Where you been, Eleanor?" I ask one day, and she starts tickling me.

"Oh, now you want to know where I been. Are you going to beat me for going out? Going out to see my lover? My teenage Latin lover?"

Eleanor puts her hands up under the front of my shirt and starts breathing in my ear and giving me her tongue. "I'm exploring the neighborhood, Johnny. You don't worry about anything. Look, I brought you a gift."

She's rubbing against me. It's another Cuban cigar. She's been decorating the apartment. We've got two rooms, a bathroom and a kitchenette. Eleanor is a great cook. It's like an insult to watch her make dinner with no space, chopping up the food right in the pan because there's no counter. Her garlic takes over the whole floor. The neighbors like our dinner smells. A couple of them have knocked, but I'm not here to make friends. I don't need these people, whoever they are, knowing my business, whatever that business may be.

I know Eleanor knows I'm depressed. And she knows that I know she knows. How I wound up with a woman this great is a mysterious thing. She always knows exactly what the problem is and how to take my mind off it. Nothing will get in the way of me and her. Two days later, she brings home a guest.

5

The first time I said "fuck" in the house my father punched me in the stomach, and I fell on the floor and couldn't breathe. "Who taught you that word?" he yelled, but I couldn't answer. "You're eight years old and you say 'fuck' in my house?"

When my wind came back, I got up and ran into my bedroom, closed the door, dove onto the bed and started crying. My mother tiptoed in, same as like when she checked to see if I was asleep at night. I always felt she was trying to be like a ghost, there but not there. I still remember the perfume she wore, a smell that made me hope she would pull me up and hold me until I disappeared from every bad thing in the world. She smelled like soap.

"You have to watch what you say around your father, Johnny. Only he can say those words in this house," she said, rocking me like a baby. I didn't feel like a baby. I wanted to grow up as fast as possible from as early as I can remember. I didn't live in a world of toys and cartoons and candy. The house was my father's house. My mother held me and told me the story about how she and he met. She was the only one who didn't call him Uncle Al. She wasn't married to the guy everybody else knew.

She was out at Coney Island with her girlfriends, the two Angelas, all of them flirting with boys and eating Nathan's on a hot summer Friday night. Coney Island had been a big part of her family for years; her grandmother had met her grandfather there when he was a pickpocket at Luna Park in 1907. She always said her grandfather separated a rich lady from a large diamond ring and proposed to my great-grandmother with it that same night while they rode the Shoot-the-Chutes. I've seen that ring — like something Elizabeth Taylor wears.

So, my mother and the Angelas are eating hot dogs and boys are all over them, but one boy is different. He comes up and says in a real gentlemanly fashion, "Ladies, if I could marry all three of you tonight, I'd be the happiest man in the world." Just like that, he had three girls.

Somehow, even though the boardwalk was packed with people, my father was able to cut lines like a king and get them in for free to every show. Professor Graf. The Headless Girl. The Pinheaded People. Tom Thumb. She still has the pictures from when all four squeezed into the photo booth, and even in those you can see he liked my mother best.

Then my mother told me the part I was always waiting for. How he had personally escorted them home at 11, first the Angelas and then her. Normally, she would never go home with a strange boy, but this night she knew something was going to happen. When they got to my mother's door, he didn't try to touch or even kiss her. He just grew very serious and said, "Someday, I'm going to marry you and we're going to have a son named John, and you're going to have everything that's in your dreams because I can give that to you."

My mother was 16 years old. She knew lots of boys, but she was scared of this one, mostly because she felt he was telling the truth. One year later, they're married and living near the racetrack, with the biggest car on the block.

"And you know what, Johnny? Even though we were married, I didn't know anything about your father. All I knew is that

I loved him. Now be a good boy and stop saying 'fuck' in the house."

———•———

I hear Eleanor say my name and open my eyes. What the fuck is that, I'm thinking, but don't say a word. My wife is standing next to a shirt the deepest color purple I've ever seen, with chest hair growing out of it like weeds on foreclosed property. I'm sunk down in the chair and blink a couple times to focus. Christ, it's some Cuban queer. It's a home invasion. The gun's in the other room. This is embarrassing.

"Eleanor, what are we doing here?"

"John, this is Cienfuegos."

Cienfuegos moves toward me, but my body language tells him to stand still, or I'll rip the chest rug right out of his shirt. So, he bends over and starts hugging me right there in the chair, laughing. He calls me Papi. I think he's wearing a wig, like a Mr. Hugo hairpiece from the shopping center. But who puts grease in a wig? He smells like cologne you'd splash on a dead relative you want to keep around the house a few extra days. He looks like a disco.

"Oh, yes! How are you? I did not mean to wake you from your living-room slumber. You looked so restful, so peaceful. Like a child, a slumbering child."

He doesn't stop. "I hope you have enjoyed the cigars. They are from the family plantation of my uncle in Cuba. Do you hate Castro? I do not, maybe a little, but, my God, here in Miami we have no choice. So, I do. He is just an old bear, Fidel. Everyone in Miami pretends to want him dead, but we are secretly very proud of how long he stays in power annoying your country. Saying 'Death to Castro' is good politics, but Castro is a true Cuban. So resilient. So strong. So virile. What is not to like?"

I'd seen "The Godfather: Part II." I knew wise guys used to run everything in Cuba. My father's cousin Anthony raced a horse called Muscle at Oriental Park in Havana in the Fifties. I knew a little bit, but I'm not tipping my hand to this fruit basket.

"Cienfuegos wants to take us to dinner, John."

Christ, Eleanor, I'm thinking, even though I've got nothing better to do.

"No Cuban food, I promise," Cienfuegos says, the first thing I've liked about him. "We are going to Joe's Stone Crabs. My treat."

Everybody calls Joe's the real Miami. How authentic can it be if everybody in there is from out of town? I smell an offer coming, a proposition. So, Eleanor has been working while I slept on my ass and got fat. I look around the dump we're living in, breathe the dead air in the Sea Breeze and decide once again to put my faith in my wife.

"What kind of name is Cienfuegos?" I ask.

"It means a hundred fires," he says, and Eleanor cracks a beer and sprays it all over the floor.

***

So restful, so peaceful. Like a child, a slumbering child. What did I look like to that guy? Soft, probably. Pot belly growing every day, a couple empty beers on the table next to my chair. Some days I didn't do enough to even call it a day.

If Eleanor was out, I'd get up, go down to the desk and borrow the manager's paper, make some eggs and sit back down in my chair. Halfway through the sports section I'm out cold, snoring. I'd wake up and drool is on the side of my chin. Then I'd make a sandwich for lunch and watch some TV. Lift weights. I was like a crazy shut-in person with a thousand cats, without the cats.

Up in New York, I was used to it getting dark early when it turned cold. Down here, though, it was hot and getting dark early. They don't have fall. They don't have winter. The leaves don't fall off the palm trees, or not when I'm looking. And what the fuck is a coconut, anyway, a fruit? By the time I got my head on straight, sometimes the sun's already going down out there, so I sit back down and wait for Eleanor. I'm the coconut.

When I had the numbers, I knew myself. When I got down here, I could be anybody, or nobody. I was back in the pack. My father would not have liked seeing this. Until they found him that morning in the alley in Gravesend behind the wheel with his pants down, he oversaw every single fucking day. So, I thought. I remember my mother looking at me very angry and scared after they called and said he was dead. She was screaming, "Are you next, John?" and she buried her face in my shirt crying and punching me in the chest over and over.

"Come on, Ma. Never." I said, trying to sound strong for her, but then I start crying, too.

"What was your father doing?" like she was in a panic. "What was he *doing*?"

I start thinking about Cienfuegos and who he might be, but that dinner at Joe's didn't come and nearly two weeks went by.

One afternoon when Eleanor is out, I can't stand the apartment and go out myself. The sun hits me, and I don't have shades on. I'm wearing the Hawaiian shirt. Two blocks down the sidewalk I realize I barely recognize anything. I don't know any people; I don't know the motels or houses, or the stores. Everybody used to know me. I start walking to get lost. I feel better than I expected. I make some turns and twenty minutes later I could have been anywhere.

I see a little store with the sign in Spanish, and I go in to get a Coke. The old man running the place is at the counter watching soccer on a TV up on the wall. A fan is spinning and clicking overhead. I start to notice things. The floor is dirty. There's a bathroom in the back. They sell mousetraps. There's a brown kid in the store, maybe 15, slipping things into his pockets. Just cheap stuff. I buy the Coke from the old man and look and see Colombia is winning, 1-0.

Outside, there's nobody around and I flip the top on the Coke and take a long swig and hiccup and feel the foam in my nose. The kid comes out and I hit him on the back of the head with the bottle and he goes down. Half the fucking Coke spills on the Hawaiian shirt. Christ, I didn't mean to hit him so hard. I felt it in my arm. It's not like he's bleeding. Maybe I got it worse than him. He's got candy, anchovies, a lighter and a new knife in his pockets. I lean on him and pin his arms in case he wants to fight me.

"You don't let no one see you when you do that, all right? How do you know I don't work in there?"

I suddenly realize I probably sound ridiculous. What the hell would I be doing working in a Latino market, a goombah? I stop talking and start thinking about my father. Would he be laughing right now? I was trying to teach the kid how to do things, but what am I doing? I got off him and gave him his stuff, and he runs away. Maybe he was bleeding a little.

Back home, Eleanor has fried grouper from the fish market. She's got the radio on, and the Drifters are singing "This Magic Moment."

And then it happened, it took me by surprise.
I knew that you felt it too, by the look in your eyes.

Eleanor slides over breaking off a piece of fish and pushing it into my mouth. She leaves her fingers in and starts singing, *"Sweeter than wine, softer than a summer night."*

I suck on her fingers. She doesn't even ask about the Coke stains. I know she wants to dance, and so do I. I feel myself against her leg, and that's good.

"We're going to Joe's tomorrow with Cienfuegos, John."

Her eyes look straight at mine. This was her plan. When we got married, I would get jealous and didn't want her to work, but I didn't marry Eleanor to be her boss. I look at men who boss their wives, and they don't trust them. They want to own them, and a man who owns his wife is alone.

6

Inside the front door at Joe's, it's crammed with people who aren't special waiting for tables. The joint is old Miami Beach and very noisy. It's fancy, but not too fancy, and they don't take reservations. It's like a chophouse with a good gimmick. I mean where else does a man wear a tie to eat crabs and creamed spinach?

They've hired all the best waiters in town. They know how to mix a cocktail. Bloody Marys with horseradish and celery and olives as big as chicken eggs. They put on their tuxes and make important people feel important and really pour it on for the tourists from cazzo buco.

They know why they've been on top so long. Because they don't change anything, ever, except the prices. The best places understand that. The Fontainebleau, the Eden Roc. This is Miami Beach. You start at the top and you don't cut corners or forget the core business. Sunshine and luxury and keep the bums out. Louie and them fucked up dropping numbers for crack and hookers. You don't see Joe's taking stone crabs off the menu to serve fish sticks.

Me and Eleanor don't go to Joe's, but they knew us right away. The maître di stopped talking to some old lady and came right over. "So happy to see you," he says. "Follow me."

It's so crowded I'm bumping into people all the way to the back, and then I see Cienfuegos rising out of his chair like an eggplant with chest hair.

He's right on Eleanor with the kisses. "You look beautiful, both of you." But he's the one wearing a scarf. I look down. I like to see a man's shoes. I don't like tassels. I don't like a man in slippers. Then his boyfriend walks in, and they kiss. On the mouth. In Joe's Stone Crabs.

I'm only going to drink beer. The boyfriend, Jimmy, looks at Cienfuegos for a long time, like he's reading his mind, and then says, "Asti Spumante." Cienfuegos smiles.

Suddenly, out of nowhere, I get focused, and it surprises me. I'm interested, and I realize I don't care what they are. I look hard at Cienfuegos and feel Eleanor's foot rubbing mine. I think it's Eleanor's. The food comes. Cienfuegos crushes the joint of a giant stone crab claw in his nutcracker.

"Your wife says you know how to play the horses, but we don't like to gamble," he says, then looks over at Jimmy. "We like to win."

"We think the world of it," Jimmy chimes in. "We like having the world on a string."

"A string we can tug," Cienfuegos says.

"A chain we can yank," Jimmy says, and they burst out laughing.

"They're just pulling your leg, John," Eleanor says.

"Crime must be fun," Cienfuegos says. "You have to be sick in your heart or mind to hurt someone, so if you don't enjoy it, you're sick and unhappy. You can't be both. It is too much for one to bear. We are a little bit sick, of course, but we prefer to be happy. So, we do bad things, but not too bad, and can live with ourselves."

That night, me and Eleanor are in bed with the lamp on by my side. We're propped up on the pillows like old people watching TV. But we're not watching TV.

"John, are you OK with this?"

"Yeah, Eleanor. Yeah." She knows I'm on edge.

If someone was going to kill me, their best chance is through Eleanor. Every single person in the room could be pointing a gun at my head, and if she said these were her friends, I'd crack a few beers and have them sit down.

That night, me and Eleanor have the exact same dream. Both of us had said goodbye at the gate and got on different planes, and after takeoff the planes start shaking and slowing down. Then the planes start diving into the ocean. In each of our dreams, we're apart and gripping the seats, and everybody starts crying and the planes just keep going down. I'm looking at this woman, a stranger, next to me. She's not my wife. I can't tell her, but what was it I needed to say? I'm trying to remember, and I see the ocean coming up close out the window. We're going to die, and I can't remember. Do I ever say what I need to say when it needs to be said, Eleanor? Why can't I remember?

Then I hear Eleanor screaming, "John!" and I jerk in the bed and feel my spirit get pulled from the plane and out of the dream, and she's sitting up, and I look at her, and we're both breathing like somebody chased us down an alley.

"I told you I love you, right?"

"Yeah, John. Always. Always."

"I was on a plane and . . ." and she doesn't want to hear anymore.

"I'm sorry, El," I said and was scared and hanging on and thinking about my father.

I think she knew that, but what was she thinking? I've got to be better making sure everything's not all about me.

7

I call the Zipper and we meet at Cuba's Good Thing for coffee, only the Zipper's drinking the water out of a coconut.

"No corkage fee, Zip?"

"It's health food, John. You've heard of health before."

The Zipper's gone past 70 but is still at the track every day. He walks hots in the morning, goes to sleep in a barn office for two hours and is down in the grandstand by first post. A stooper, a carrier pigeon, a pickpocket, and a gambling addict. Carrier pigeon is most important. He doesn't do much for himself, but he's a messenger, the connective tissue between people who want to talk to each other, but not even on the phone. He's quiet, but not like Big Al Raymond. Just the opposite. He wants to appear harmless, part of the local color.

On dark days, when there's no live racing, Zipper's humming and watering the flowerpots outside the shithole dorms where they stick the Mexicans. He does little favors, like jumping up to grab napkins if you spill coffee in the track kitchen.

Getting old made even better cover for his rackets. He used to have a big head of white hair, but baldness mowed the lawn right down the middle. Now white hair grows out of his ears. He greases his hair back on the sides. His face is cracked from the sun. He's got one tooth — one tooth — and sometimes I want to yank it right out of his head. He squints indoors but sees perfect. You know a limp is coming. It's just a matter of time. You would never know Zip is an inside man. His body is now a perfect disguise.

My father bought the Zipper a houseboat at a marina outside Hallandale for something he did that no one talks about. Zip moved in and would come out in the morning wearing a little white skipper's cap like Count Basie. He got tired of the bumping against the dock all night and sank his home for the insurance. In February, he lost everything trying to crush a horse named Tustunugee in the Fountain of Youth. Going from Remington Park in Oklahoma to one of the biggest Derby prep races is like trying to fly a paper plane to the Moon.

The horse actually made the lead and ran the first quarter mile in under 23 seconds. Knowing Zip, a little tinkle came out. At the top of the lane Tustunugee melted like a chocolate horse in a heatwave. What was Zip thinking? Tustunugee's odds were 435-1. It's not the fucking movies.

Coconut water dribbling down his shirt, the Zipper looks at me like a schoolteacher talking to a bad kid he can't help liking.

"I don't know what this is you got going, Johnny. Do you?"

What am I going to say? It's Eleanor's idea? Cienfuegos' plan is crazy, so I must be too. I don't feel like I'm making choices; they're just happening. I was taught not to leave things to chance, but here we go.

———◦———

At his stucco palace on Bayshore Drive, Cienfuegos shows me the gun he made, only it doesn't shoot bullets. He holds it up to my head, and like he's singing to an infant says, "I know you trust me. Yes, you do," and pulls the trigger. My head stays up there.

"Come with me, now," he says. "We go outside."

On the patio, Cienfuegos has two yappy dogs that look like bedroom slippers. They're out there stupid with the heat. Cienfuegos points the gun at one with a red ribbon on its head — just points it — and the thing starts whimpering and runs around in a circle. The dog's literally weeping, and a little shit squirts out.

"The human hears 20 hertz to 20 kilohertz," Cienfuegos says. "The horse hears much better, 14 hertz to 25 kilohertz. My poor baby, Chumo, hears up to 47,000 kilohertz, so the gun really hurts him. The hertz hurts."

Cienfuegos starts laughing like a pig squeals. This guy is in love with himself.

"So, we shoot the horse with 25 kilohertz if he is winning," Cienfuegos says. "He will believe a screaming witch has come for him. Whoever is on his back better have good insurance. The best part is, if the horse is going to lose, we don't need to do anything."

I ask a dumb question. "How's it going to look with you pointing a gun at the horses at the track?"

"Ah, this is a good question." Cienfuegos opens his pocketbook and pulls out a binoculars case.

"The gun is in here, too."

He slips the binoculars out of the case. They look like ordinary black racing binoculars, but then he takes off the lens cap and turns them around.

"See?"

Inside, the eye pieces look like tiny machines.

"I built the ultrasonic transducers myself," Cienfuegos says. "And you know how I learned to do this? In a book! Imagine! And you know what this makes me? Amazing, right? Come on, John. You are impressed."

I look at the dogs. They're both unconscious on the patio.

The Zipper's job is to make a little scene, a little distraction. Nothing big, maybe just some shouting or punch a grandstand drunk; just enough that not every eye is going to be on the horses in the lane. Just other stuff happening, you know? The stewards upstairs are going to see the race, and they've got replay, but what are they going to do? The horse spooks. The jock falls off. End of story. They're not going to see the gay Cuban at the rail with a Buck Rogers ray gun in his binoculars.

"Cienfuegos," I say, "no purple. No scarves. Look like just another bum."

"OK, I pretend I am you."

I get back in my car. On the passenger seat next to me is a briefcase holding $15,000 in cash.

It can't just be any race; we have to wait. The game is to take down a 1-to-5 shot, a horse that looks like Secretariat on rocket fuel. A stone-cold lock. Betting against this horse would be like putting out a cigarette on the pope.

It has to be on one of the biggest days of the meet with a big crowd. The more money in the pools, the less chance officials get a sniff of us.

Eleanor and I, we do the betting. When the gate opens, there could be $200,000 or more in all the pools. We're going to be hitting the win pool, the exactas, and the triple. If a bridge jumper drops suitcases of cash into the show pool, no problem. We'll take that, too.

Every five minutes, from the end of the prior race up to ours, Eleanor and I send it in — on self-service terminals, not with the tellers. No one needs to meet us. We use multiple vouchers. If we bet it all in one lump, the movement will be noticeable on the tote board and in the back office. This way, it all gets lost in the flow of the action.

Jimmy, meantime, will be at home, playing through a phone betting account. By the time the windows close, we'll have pumped about $30,000 into bets on the primary horses other than the favorite, about 15 percent of the total pool. We're not looking to draw attention; we're looking to make money. The favorite will have taken about 70 percent of the money wagered. We're backing up our truck to collect the lion's share of that.

This is not exactly what I was expecting when we got to Bal Harbour. Now, me and Eleanor are living in a dump, I'm wearing Hawaiian shirts, and we're planning to drop a horse with a ray gun.

I'm back with the Zip having a Bloody Mary at Billy's. We're sitting by the Intracoastal, outside. He's got a banana daiquiri and is opening and closing the little umbrella like it's a puzzle. Like he's 4 years old.

"This is well made, John."

Down the row of tables, a pelican is on the deck locked on a man eating a shrimp cocktail. The bird's rocking back and forth like he's on junk and needs a shrimp bad. I start laughing.

"What?"

"Nothing, Zip."

"Come on. What?"

I lean across the table and smile at him. "This is fun. That's all."

8

One Sunday, a couple weeks before they found him, my father said he was taking me for a ride. We drove out to Long Island, to a little Italian neighborhood called Manorhaven on the North Shore. He wanted to eat a garbage pie at a pizza joint called Andy's. I don't know how he heard about this place, but he knew what he was doing.

There was an Italian bread bakery right next door and Our Lady of Fatima right next to that. Just a beautiful pie, and you could smell the smoke in the crust that would bubble up and crack. Sausage, pepperoni, mushrooms, fresh garlic, red peppers, basil. Garbage pie. Even anchovies. We ate the whole thing, just the two of us, sitting in the car parked at a marina watching boats come in and the sun go down.

"You know something, John? I don't know if the world is beautiful or terrible. I really don't. Tonight is beautiful. Your mother is beautiful. Sometimes I'm terrible. And I have no idea how people get to be who they get to be. One guy becomes the president. One guy's picking up garbage. One guy's Black. Another guy's Italian. One guy's a Jew. It's all a crapshoot; fucking chaos."

I didn't think about it then, but after what happened, looking back, he was being eaten alive. He always liked to be in control. He wanted everything just right. When he worked, variables and surprises meant possible trouble. Planning meant success. My mother never worried about him. Why should she? He always took care of everything. But control has its price. Just going to Long Island for that pizza was out of line for him. Men are animals. They can't stay in the cage. My father hid his need for freedom — whatever that meant — and it killed him.

When we got to Florida, I was practically nothing. I let myself let Eleanor take over and now I'm floating. My father was right — life is fucking chaos, but it's like the Cyclone at Coney Island. It scares the shit out of you, and your only choice is to trust it's not going to fly off the rails. The problem is when you get on a ride and you know the rails are loose. Three weeks after they found my father, my mother moved in with her cousins in Schenectady. Her hair turned white and one day she walked into traffic.

We forgot to take napkins and my dad tried to wipe his face with the wax paper inside the box. He had pizza grease all over his mouth.

"Give me your sleeve," he said, pulling on me, and we started laughing.

He stretched in the car like he might take a nap after four slices and looked out at the water. It might have been the last time we were alone together.

"I should have gotten us a boat, John," he said and looked at me. "Should I have gotten a boat?"

It's the second week in March, the time of year Gulfstream Park is the only racetrack that matters. Every big-shot trainer and degenerate gambler on the East Coast is in South Florida. After three weeks of pouring over the entries, just the kind of horse we've been waiting for appears like a blessed vision — Our Lady of the Racing Form.

Our horse's name is Nunca te Detengas. Cienfuegos tells me it means never slow down in Spanish. She raced three times in Chile and won all three by 35 lengths. Some swinging hedge fund dicks bought her for

$400,000 and brought her up here. She won her first try at Gulfstream by 10 lengths in an allowance race and missed the track record by two-fifths.

The newspaper guys are going nuts for her. One even compared her to Canonero II, who came up from Venezuela and won the Derby. Chile, Venezuela — what's the difference, right?

We pull into the parking lot at Gulfstream and Eleanor leans over and whispers in my ear, "You want a little something right here?"

She slides her hand between my legs and starts to rub. Jesus, either this whole thing is turning her on or she's going un po 'pazzo, a little crazy. She sure doesn't look scared. We're both wearing sunglasses that practically cover our faces, and I don't even know where she got our get-ups. We look like the couple you avoid on a cruise ship.

It's Florida Derby Day and the place is already packed at 2 o'clock. The less time we spend here, the less chance people notice us. People might notice us, but I don't think they're going to pay us any attention. Still, under the sunglasses my eyes are looking everywhere. There are beautiful girls with dark tans wearing short dresses. Men are buried in their racing forms and looking up every time a girl walks by. Kids are running wild. Even if they have parents, they may never see them again.

We're focused on a race called The Orchid. It's a mile and three-eighths on the grass for fillies and mares 4 years old and up. Nunca te Detengas is even-money on the morning line. The linemaker was being polite. She's so scary, only four other horses are entered against her, which makes the race perfect for us because it eliminates the variables when we bet. One of her opponents has never even run on grass before; another hasn't won on it in five tries. So, the other two — good horses, but not that good — are our primary betting focus.

When the race before ours is official, the odds for the Orchid are posted for the first time on the tote board. Nunca te Detengas opens at 1-5.

We've got the $15,000 from Cienfuegos and $15,000 of our own money. That's a lot of cash to be walking around with anywhere, let alone a racetrack. We're inside the clubhouse betting area. The air conditioning is blowing. I see two guys get into it on my left. One has beer all over his shirt, and he punches the other guy, much larger, right in the chest. The big guy barely shifts, and then they're on the floor rolling around trying to kill each other. I see a security guard, who does not give one shit, check his watch, so I relax.

Eleanor and I move toward the betting machines. We loiter around for five minutes talking about getting pizza at Mama Jennie's. We bought fancy pagers for the day, and I feel mine go off. The fuck?

It's the Zipper and the screen says: "Track apron."

Then it goes off again. "Finish line."

"Eleanor, I gotta see the Zip."

"Give me the cash, John."

For a second, I look hard into Eleanor's face to see if I can see something without saying something. I don't know what I'm expecting from her, but "Give me the cash, John" came out like it didn't take much thinking.

"Beep me back soon," she says. "'Y' for OK, 'N' for not."

I don't answer. I don't even look around. I pull the thick stack of bills out of my little bag and push them into her pocketbook and walk out. Down at the rail, Zip's standing in a sea of tourists and drunken bums.

"Just walk out to the lot," he says. "Let's go."

So we go. I take out the beeper and type 'N' and 'Car' to Eleanor. Then I spot Cienfuegos about twenty feet away in a dirty T-shirt and jeans walking through the crowd to the rail up by the eighth pole. Printed on the front of his shirt is a pack of teenage boys. Jesus.

"Zip, what's Menudo?"

"Come on, John, walk."

Cienfuegos doesn't see us. He's got the binoculars. I don't know what's going on, but for the first time since I loaded it, I feel the weight of my gun inside the left pocket of my coat.

We're walking to my car at Gulfstream Park, but I'm thinking about the time in Staten Island when I shot a guy I knew, a neighborhood guy, in the leg, in a parking lot. That wasn't part of my work, but I heard through friends that he had been saying bad things about us. I knew if it got to the wrong ears, Louie would have him killed. So, I just shot him in the leg to quiet him down. I didn't want him to get hurt badly, you know? I never heard anyone scream like that in my life. The bullet went straight through the fender of the car behind him. I walked over and gave him a pain pill I had brought along.

"Take this," I said, and he reached his shaking hand up and pushed it into his mouth. "I'm not your friend but recognize this was a favor. I've already called an ambulance and the police. Tell them you were mugged and give a crazy description. If you don't, you won't even make it out of the hospital because friends there are expecting you."

I put my hand on his shoulder. "Does it hurt?" He was sweating and shook his head yes. "Wait a couple minutes; I swear an ambulance is coming. Next time you see me, say hello, OK?"

"Johnny."

It's Zip. We're at the car. I spaced out. I check my watch. Three minutes to post. I turn back and here comes Eleanor, in a trot.

"Give me the keys, John," she says, and I want to laugh. Eleanor's calling all the shots now. I mean, look at my wife. Wow. That's what I'm thinking. We pull out and head up the road.

"So, what's happening here?" I finally ask, after we drive in silence two miles north on Biscayne Boulevard. We don't have any business in this direction. Now Zip starts laughing in the back seat. Eleanor pulls into Cuba's Good Thing and puts it in park. She pulls out a handful of betting tickets and passes them back. Zip leans forward and puts a hand on each of our shoulders.

"Be in touch, kids," he says and gets out.

My beeper goes off. It's Cienfuegos. One word: "Launched."

I picture the jockey flying off Nunca te Detengas in slow-motion and being trampled to death by the horses behind him. Next message: "Line One." That's the row of mutuel tellers where we're supposed to all meet and start getting paid.

Well, that's not happening.

"Looks like we won, El," I say.

Eleanor pulls over at a bus stop and hands me her beeper. "In the garbage, John."

They're nice beepers. I get out, toss them and get back in. She kisses me on the mouth, hard and quick like when we first started going together.

My wife has bet all our money, and we've got a year to cash in. She's also taken and bet all Cienfuegos's money, and he's going to have to get over it. We've got about a hundred grand.

My mind is spinning trying to figure this thing out. Clearly, I'm the stooge, Cienfuegos the mark, and Zip, well, Zip is always the facilitator. My double-crossing wife had made me perfectly trustworthy to Cienfuegos because I knew about as much as he did — which was nothing — and I guess I wasn't the only one drinking coffee with Zip at Cuba's Good Thing.

So now, Eleanor is some kind of criminal mastermind, and we're on the run. I'm quiet in the car for a minute, and she's looking over at me while driving.

"John?"

I think about how my mother only knew so much about my father before he reached a dead end in Gravesend. What choice did she have but to keep her faith in him? I realized my faith in Eleanor wasn't based on anything she had been doing since Cienfuegos danced in the door, but everything that came before. Trust counts in past performances, just like when you're betting horses, and you choose to believe in someone because it takes trust to win, to make things work, to stay alive. If you want a future, you've got to trust and keep going. That's the opposite of mob thinking — trust no one — but you know what? That's not me. OK, that is me, but . . .

"Johnny."

Eleanor pulls into a used car lot, and a man walks out to meet us. She hands him our keys. Sitting out there with the engine running is a white Ford Explorer with all our clothes and a few other things in the back. I look at the grill as we walk over. New York plates.

"It's used, John, but gently," Eleanor says, handing me the keys. "No bill of sale; just title and registration."

We climb in and pull out. Eleanor turns on the radio to an oldies station and starts humming. It's the Drifters, her favorite. Me, I just drive. Twenty miles up the road, it sinks in. I've got it all. My wife is literally my partner in crime.

"How you feelin', John?"

"Good, Eleanor. I feel good," and the laughter rolls out of me until I'm practically choking.

"Good," Eleanor says, punching me in the arm and rolling down the window. "You know something, Johnny? You were right all along about this. We're getting out of Florida."

About the Author

John Scheinman grew up on Long Island and is a writer and editor living in Baltimore. The last turf beat writer for *The Washington Post*, he is a two-time Eclipse Award winner for excellence in writing about thoroughbred racing. His piece "Memories of a Master" was named a notable sports story in "The Best American Sports Writing 2015" anthology. His headline writing and general reporting has been honored by the Maryland-Delaware-D.C. Press Association and Society of Professional Journalists. His sketch comedy has been performed at the Warehouse and Source theaters in Washington, D.C. and Theatre Odyssey in Sarasota, Florida. He made his standup comedy debut in 2019 at the DC Improv Comedy Club. A graduate of American University, he studied writing with Pulitzer Prize-winning poet Henry Taylor and improvisational comedy and performance at The Theatre Lab in Washington. He began his journalism career at *The Ring*, "The Bible of Boxing."

CPSIA information can be obtained
at www.ICGtesting.com
Printed in the USA
BVHW030807010721
610937BV00002B/76